Amelia and Gabby

Ready or Not: Here We Come!

By

Lia Marino

Illustrated by

Stacy Evans

Amelia and Gabby: Ready or Not: Here We Come!

Warren Publishing, Inc.

ISBN 978-1-886057-27-2
Library of Congress Control Number: 2008933772

Printed in China

www.Warrenpublishing.net

There is a special bond between sisters,
a friendship that outlasts any other.

This book is dedicated to my daughters, Amelia
and Gabby, to my sister Lynn, and to sisters
everywhere. A special thanks to my husband,
Anthony, for his love and support.

- L. M.

The day I learned how to roller blade
is a day I will never forget.
In July, my sister Gabby and I,
along with our parents,
traveled to Ohio to visit our family
and celebrate our birthdays.
Since our birthdays are only five days apart,
Gabby and I always celebrate them together.

One year, our dad bought us roller blades, about 47
pads for every part of our bodies,
and of course helmets. Couldn't forget those!
The tissue paper flew as we sat in the driveway
ripping open all the boxes.
It was so exciting!
Once we opened everything,
it seemed to take hours to put on all our gear.

Our Aunt Lynn already knew how to roller blade
and she was determined to teach us.
She was decked out in her gear too.
We all looked **fantastic** from head to toe.

However, we soon found out there was more to it than looking good.
There was a lot of falling involved in learning how to roller blade.
Someone should have invented one more pad for my _____,
if you know what I mean!
I kept landing on mine over and over.

Going straight on a flat surface was pretty easy,
but going down hill…that was another story.
Our grandparents' driveway was flat, but their street
had a slight slope that led to the cul-de-sac.

You could really go fast on roller blades,
even when you didn't want to, and believe me, we didn't want to.
Until we learned how to stop,
it seemed like we were racing at 100 miles per hour.
I think learning to ride a bike was much easier!

Finally, after a lot of trying and crashing, I got it.
Gabby yelled, "Yeah, Amelia! You got it!"
Gabby got her stride going soon after, too.
She could finally let go of Aunt Lynn's hand.

The three of us skated around the cul-de-sac over and over.
We had a great time that day with Aunt Lynn!
The day I learned how to roller blade
is a day I will never forget,
like the day my sister got Mrs. Gambill for the 4th grade.

The day my sister got
Mrs. Gambill for the 4th grade
is a day I will never forget.
I was sooooo happy for her!
I remember 4th grade so well...

Mrs. Gambill was my **favorite**,
I mean my **favorite** teacher,
and my mother's, too.
Mom was her classroom helper.

Mrs. Gambill had very strict guidelines and class rules.
Our desks were checked for neatness,
we walked down the halls very quietly in straight lines,
papers needed to be in her box first thing
and if your name was not on it,
it was an automatic ten points off.
Don't bother trying to explain!

Mrs. Gambill was serious and fun at the same time.
She looked like a classic schoolteacher.
Her hair was always in place,
she wore big eyeglasses,
and every holiday she wore a special sweater
or vest for the occasion.
She brightened up the classroom with her holiday spirit.
All kids should have a "Mrs. Gambill" at least once.

Fourth grade was very tough,
with way more work than third grade.
TESTS, **TESTS**, and **MORE TESTS**,
homework assignments up to the ceiling,
and if you didn't have a book
to read at all times…
your goose was cooked!

We spent a lot of time learning how to write a story
using descriptive words to make it more interesting.
If you started too many sentences with "I,"
you might as well have made a run for it!

We studied everything there was to know about
North Carolina too.

My favorite section was on lighthouses.
We learned about all of them
and had to build one for a project.
I loved that project!
Mrs. Gambill always encouraged
the best from us,
and we tried our best
to give it to her.

Gabby's eyes lit up when she saw her name
on Mrs. Gambill's class list,
and when Mrs. Gambill found out
she was getting Gabby in her class,
she was just as excited!

Gabby knew she was getting a sweet deal...
a great teacher and her mom as the classroom helper.
Gabby is going to love having our mom in the classroom.
Of course, if Gabby could take our mom to school with her everyday,
she would! The day my sister got Mrs. Gambill for the 4th grade is a
day I will never forget, like the day I got my braces.

The day I got my braces is a day I will never forget.
Here I was, already so adorable, except for a teensy,
weensy space between my two front teeth.
It was affecting my adorableness,
so I had to get them a little smooshed together.

However, smooshing, I found out, required braces.
The mere thought of gluing tiny, shiny, metal brackets
onto my teeth was not very appealing to me,
but for some reason, it was to my little sister, Gabby.

Like clockwork, every six months from the time she lost her last
baby tooth, Gabby asked when she was getting her braces put on.
As her big sister, I was obligated to inform her
about the obvious problems with braces.
For instance, no chewing gum or hard candy, bits of food that can
get stuck in them, and of course the school picture-day dilemma;
should I smile and say "cheese" and show my metal mouth, or not?

There was, however, a small upside for my troubles.
My spirits perked up when I was presented with a board of
colored samples of braces.
"Colors to match the occasion? What a good idea," I thought.
I could see it now, red for Christmas, orange for Halloween
and green for Saint Patrick's Day to name a few.
I would always look festive.

Luckily, the smooshing process only took one year.
Switching colors at each check-up helped make braces fun,
in a make-the-most-of-the-situation kind of way.
When the braces came off, my teeth felt smooth and a little weird,
but it was sooooo worth it!
Now as for Gabby, her long awaited wish to finally get
her braces on was about to be granted.
Filled with excitement, Gabby arrived at her appointment
with a big smile on her face.
The day she had been waiting for had arrived.

We thought for sure the little fashionista would pick her favorite color to brighten up her teeth, but she surprised us all and got plain, shiny metal brackets. There was little discomfort, no panic attacks about food stuck in them or picture day dilemmas. Even though she didn't take advantage of changing colors to match the occasion, and she smiled with her braces showing for picture day, it didn't affect her adorableness one bit!

The day I got my braces is a day I will never forget, like the day I...

Well, I'll tell you all about that later!

The End